Disney
Winnie the Pooh

Play All Day Songs

Oh, hello. It's me, Winnie the Pooh. I have some very dear friends who are going to sing some songs about friendship and fun things to do. Would you like to sing along?

Story Reader™

publications international, ltd.

Hum de dum dum. It's a hummy sort of day outside, the sort of day when, if you meet a friend, you're very likely to begin humming a hum together. That's the sort of day I like very much.

Rig-a-Jig-Jig

When Piglet and I spend a morning together,
it's always a very happy morning indeed.

The More We Get Together

The more we get to-geth - er, to -
geth - er, to - geth - er, the more we get to -
geth - er the hap -pi - er we'll be. For
your friends are my friends and my friends are
your friends. The more we get to - geth - er the
hap -pi - er we'll be!

If you want to be near some bees, it's rather helpful to climb a tree. Which is what Roo and I have done, as you can see.

The Bear

The oth-er day (the oth-er day) I met a

bear (I met a bear), a great big bear (a great big

bear) a way up there (a way up there). The oth-er

day I met a bear, _____

___ a great big bear a way up

there!

Tigger rather likes bouncing in puddles, especially the muddy ones. He says that the "muddliest" ones are almost always the "puddliest" ones, too.

If You're Happy

If you're hap-py and you know it make a

splash. If you're hap-py and you know it make a

splash. If you're hap-py and you know it then your

face will sure-ly show it. If you're hap-py and you know it make a

splash!

Floating and fishing with a friend are two of my very favorite things. Unless, of course, there is honey for lunch. Then that is my most favorite thing of all.

Row Your Boat

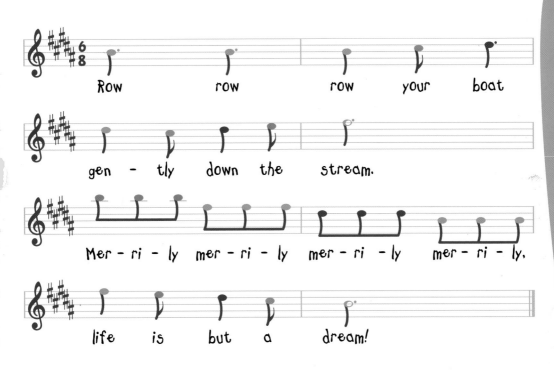

Row   row   row   your   boat

gen – tly   down   the   stream.

Mer – ri – ly mer-ri – ly mer – ri – ly mer-ri – ly,

life   is   but   a   dream!

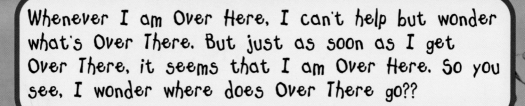

Whenever I am Over Here, I can't help but wonder what's Over There. But just as soon as I get Over There, it seems that I am Over Here. So you see, I wonder where does Over There go??

The Bear Went Over the Mountain

The bear went o-ver the moun - tain, the bear went o-ver the moun - tain, the bear went o-ver the moun - tain to see what he could see. To see what he could see, to see what he could see. The oth - er side of the moun - tain, the oth - er side of the moun - tain, the oth - er side of the moun - tain was all that he could see!

Ice skating with friends is a very friendly thing to do. But sometimes, it seems that it is a rather falling thing to do, too.

Girls and Boys, Come Out to Play

Girls and boys, come out to play. The

moon does shine as bright as day. The

air is crisp and the snow is nice.

Come join your friends skat - ing on the ice!

When playing wintry games, it is often rather useful to play them in wintry weather.

Dear Old Pals

Dear old pals, jol-ly old pals,

al - ways to-geth-er in all kinds of weath-er.

Rain or snow or for-ty be - low,

give me for friend-ship my jol-ly old pals!

I do believe it's time to do my stoutness exercises. Hum de dum. Hum de dum. Oh bother, my tummy rumbled!

Pooh Bear

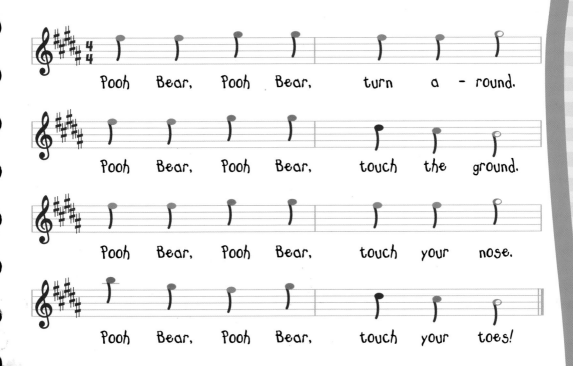

Pooh Bear, Pooh Bear, turn a - round.

Pooh Bear, Pooh Bear, touch the ground.

Pooh Bear, Pooh Bear, touch your nose.

Pooh Bear, Pooh Bear, touch your toes!

If you must play in the rain, which you must if it happens to be raining when you happen to be playing, then it's ever so much friendlier with two.

Rain, Rain, Go Away

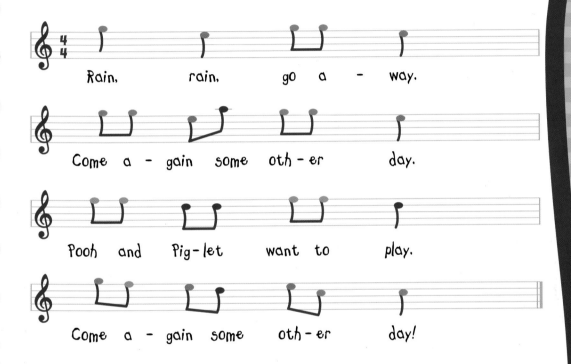

Rain,   rain,   go a - way.

Come a - gain some oth - er   day.

Pooh and Pig - let   want to   play.

Come a - gain some   oth - er   day!

Six Little Ducks

Six lit-tle ducks that   I   once knew,

fat ones, skin-ny ones   fair   ones too. But the

one lit-tle duck with the feath-er on his back,

he led the oth-ers with a quack, quack, quack!